fimbles ™

Wig

D0996042

Florrie and Baby Pom were very busy.
"Hello!" called Bessie. "What are you doing?"
"Party! Party!" said Baby Pom.

"We've made pretend food – twig biscuits, leaf cake and mud porridge," said Florrie.

"Yummy, my favourites," said Bessie.

"Crackers! Apples!" said Baby Pom.

"Oh yes, we have those, too," said Florrie.
"Would you like to come to the party, Bessie?"
"I'd love to," said Bessie. "Can I bring Ribble?"
Baby Pom jumped up and down. "Yes, yes, Ribbly Bibbly!"

"There's lots of food," said Florrie, so Bessie flew off to find Fimbo and Rockit.

Bessie found Fimbo and Rockit playing football.
"Good one!" called Fimbo. "You're great at this, Rockit!"

As Fimbo ran after the ball, his nose started to twitch.

The bubbles from the Bubble Fall went "Ping! Ping!"

He was getting the Fimbling Feeling.

"I can feel a twinkling,
I can hear a sound,
It's telling me there's something
Waiting to be found!
Where is it? Where is it?
What could it be?
I think it might be over there.
Let's go and see!"

What Fimbo saw was something pink and sparkly.

"It's a hedgehog," said Rockit, hopping up.
"Pleased to meet you, Mr Hedgehog," he said.

"Hedgehogs aren't pink and sparkly," said Bessie, laughing.
"Here's a clue – you can wear this on your head."

"Jiggedy jig, you found a wig!" laughed Rockit.

Fimbo put the wig on Rockit's head.
It was so big that it covered him.

"You look like a hedgehog now!" Bessie joked.

"Now it's my turn," said Fimbo.
"Close your eyes."

Rockit closed his eyes, and when he opened them...
"Who are you?" he asked, surprised.

"Guess!" Fimbo giggled.

"You look so different! I don't think Florrie and Baby Pom will recognize you," said Bessie.

"Let's go and see!" said Fimbo.

"I'm going to call you 'Rimbo'!" said Rockit.

"Hello, Rimbo!" laughed Bessie.

Fimbo and Rockit found Florrie and Baby Pom at the Busy Base, putting the finishing touches to their tea party.
"Ask Florrie and Baby Pom if you can bring a special friend to tea," Fimbo whispered to Rockit.

"Who's the special friend?" asked Rockit.

"Me, of course – Rimbo!" explained Fimbo.

"Hello Rockit," said Florrie.
"Are you coming to our party?"

"Ooh, yes, please," replied Rockit.
"And can I bring a special friend?"
"Who?" asked Florrie.

"Fim... I mean Rimbo," said Rockit, turning round and introducing Fimbo in the pink sparkly wig.
Florrie gasped in surprise. "Oh, hello, Rimbo. Nice to meet you."

The Crumble Crackers and apples on the party table looked delicious. Fimbo wanted to start eating straightaway, but Florrie wanted to sing her party song first.

Then Baby Pom wanted to play a game.

"Tiptoe, tiptoe?"
she asked the others.
"Good idea!" said Florrie
and Rockit.
"Let's all play Tiptoe Time."

"No," said Fimbo loudly in his normal voice, before remembering that he was in disguise.

He quickly followed the others to the Purple Meadow, pretending to be Rimbo.

As they walked, Florrie kept looking at Fimbo in a puzzled way.

Fimbo was 'it' first in the game of Tiptoe Time. He stood with his back to the others, and they crept up quietly behind him.

They had to try and touch Fimbo before he turned round and saw them moving.

But all Fimbo could think about was eating his favourite food, Crumble Crackers.

So he let Baby Pom catch him quickly, hoping that tea would come next.

Now it was Baby Pom's turn to be 'it'.

  While the others tiptoed up behind her,
Fimbo crept away in the opposite direction.
  "Cracker time," he whispered, and he was just
about to grab one, when he heard a voice behind him.

"Rimbo, if you're hungry try this yummy mud porridge."
Fimbo jumped in surprise. It was Florrie.
"Erm..." stuttered Fimbo, "I really just want a Crumble Cracker."
"I'm saving those for Fimbo – they're his favourites," said Florrie.

Fimbo really wanted to eat the Crumble Crackers, so he took off the wig!

"Oh, hello, Fimbo," said a surprised Florrie. "It's you!"

"Can I please have a cracker now?" said Fimbo.

"OK," laughed Florrie.

Baby Pom picked up the
pink wig and put it on.
"Hello wig!" she whispered.

"I wonder who that is?"
giggled Florrie.
"You can be Baby Fom!"
Everyone laughed.

"Fom, Fom!" squealed Pom.